Building my Self-

eSTEAM

in Science

by Yasmine Daniels, PhD

Find your chemistry, create your destiny!

Dr. Classy Daniels Chemist

12-5-20

volume 1

Dedication

To my son

Jaxon H. Gustave

Acknowledgement

Without God, I would be lost. I am eternally grateful to the Almighty Father for always uplifting me and keeping me victorious throughout my journey. With gratitude, I also acknowledge the countless individuals who have helped to shape my upbringing; my husband, parents, grandparents, siblings, relatives, friends and mentors. I am extremely grateful to Dr. Spiro Alexandratos who mentored me throughout my collegiate and graduate career and who has remained a positive role model in my life.

To my team who helped bring the characters in this book to life; Terrance Smith and Heddrick McBride, thank you. Thank you, also, to the wonderful group of illustrators at HH-Pax.

Table of Contents

Preface

When I first became a mom, I understood for the first time in my life how much influence and responsibility parents had in defining the quality of education and depth of experience afforded to their children. Before that, in my role as an aunt, Godmother, Coach, Professor and mentor, my duties and responsibilities were far more limited.

What I experienced as a child, a student, a mentor and now parent, has made me realize that without support, encouragement, and reassurance, the road to success is a long and bitter one. Those who provided support, played a huge role in shaping my life today and I will always remember how important it is to reinvest into those coming behind me.

While the story in this book is fictional, certain events within it reflect a lot of my own experiences. It combines real life with fiction and highlights some of the struggles many youth face in school. The main character, Charissma, is a lot like me. It is why I named her after me. Charissma is my middle name. Her story is meant to inspire and empower. Having faced numerous obstacles along her journey, she manages to persevere with the support and help of those who care for her the most.

This work of art is dedicated to my son, Jaxon Gustave, who reignited my creativity and fueled my passion to teach and nurture children.

Although the ideas for this book are based on my own experiences, the story was brought to life through contributions by Heddrick McBride, Terrence Smith and HH-Pax.

Introduction

Five high school juniors embark on a journey to plan a unique, surprise Sweet 16th birthday party for their fellow classmate at Huntwood High School.

The unsuspecting classmate is 15 year old Charissma Jackson, who recently got promoted to the 11th grade honors class. Honors students at Huntwood High School are required to take more advanced classes and the coursework is often taught at a quicker pace. Since being promoted, Charissma has struggled to meet the demands of the advanced academic load, especially in the subject areas of Science, Technology, Engineering, Art and Mathematics, also referred to as STEAM. Charissma feels helpless because she is too embarrassed to ask her new classmates for help and her old classmates are unfamiliar with the new coursework. Charissma quickly becomes discouraged and considers giving up and returning to her old class where the work was not as difficult. Her 16th birthday is approaching but Charissma barely remembers and shows almost no excitement leading up to the day because she is very overwhelmed with her studies.

At home, her family gives very little support with her schoolwork. She comes from a family that is not too familiar with STEAM subjects and they are unable to give her much support. Her single mother works two jobs, one as a janitor at the local hospital and the other as a part-time waitress at the local diner. Ms. Jackson cannot wait for Charissma to graduate high school so that she can get a job and help out with the bills. Ms. Jackson never went to college and thinks that her money is better spent paying bills than paying for Charissma to pursue wild dreams in college. Charissma is the eldest of three siblings and when she is not at school, she spends most of her free time taking care of her two younger siblings, while her mother works.

Charissma has dreams of finishing high school and going off to college and medical school. Although her mother would never be able to afford her college and medical school tuition, Charissma knows that becoming a doctor would be her ticket out. As a doctor, she would not only be doing what she always dreamed of, but she would also be making enough money to pay off all of her mother's bills and help her younger siblings through college.

Shortly after Charissma's friends throw her the surprise birthday party, she gets a huge boost in confidence and her "self-eSTEAM" which is a play on the word "self-esteem". Her friends remind her of some important lessons taking place throughout the story:

(1) Don't ever feel intimidated by something you may not understand.
(2) Our everyday activities are a big part of STEAM education.
(3) The best way to learn is to make learning fun.
(4) There is always someone willing to lend a helping hand. You just need to know where to look.

The reader gets to see how friendship, learning and fun are portrayed through the life experiences of the STEAM friends.

Chapter 1

Exploding Volcanoes, Slime and STEAM

"Welcome! Welcome!" Shaunice Wallace called out as she stood where all could see her, "to Huntwood High's annual STEAM Honors open house. The exploding volcano presentation will begin in 15 minutes and you won't want to miss it! See you at the Science booth, in FIFTEEEEEEEN minutes!"

The school's gym was filled with excited students and parents wandering from one booth to the next, admiring the different demonstrations on display. Word got around school that this year there would be amazing robots, flying drones, cool video games and there were even some dance performers at the Open House.

Huntwood High was one of the most popular schools around because there were always fun and exciting school activities offered to the students.

Shaunice and her Science classmates were in charge of the Science booth and spent the morning waving everyone over to show off their experiments. The school fair was in full swing with tables and platforms throughout the gym, showing off the students' work.

Normally, Shaunice was always full of energy and excitement when it came to school activities, especially when it involved science but for some reason, she didn't feel like herself today. On the outside she smiled and welcomed folks to the event, but on the inside, she was exhausted. Her science teacher, Mr. Shapiro, put her in charge of the Science booth because she was an A+ science student and he knew he could rely on her to keep things running smoothly. Shaunice was also a cheerleader and carried her cheerful school spirit to all school events.

"Alright guys, Huntwood High on three," whispered Shaunice to her classmates, as they touched hands in a huddle behind the science table, just before they started the volcano demo. "One, two—"

"Hey there, Shaunice!" interrupted her best friend Charissma. "Is there anything I can help you guys out with?" Charissma was standing at the front of the booth with Mr. Shapiro where the slime and elephant toothpaste demonstrations were oozing.

"Shaunice," Mr. Shapiro said, "I noticed you're limping a little bit. Did you get hurt?"

"I really don't feel well today," she replied, "but it's nothing to worry about. The show will go on and I will see it through!" Shaunice did not want to disappoint Mr. Shapiro, so she continued to push through the pain she was feeling in her leg.

At a nearby table Shaunice could hear two students talking to each other loudly. One asked, "So what's STEAM anyway? Is that like the stuff that comes from a train? I really don't get what that stuff has to do with this open house."

Shaunice smiled to herself and walked over to them. "Hey guys, I'm Shaunice. I noticed you looking over at our table. You should come check it out."

"I don't get it, what do science experiments have to do with steam trains?" one of the students asked.

Shaunice readily answered, "Well actually, STEAM stands for Science, Technology, Engineering and Mathematics. The STEAM program helps us bring students from different subjects together and allows us to be creative while solving problems together and doing really cool projects. It really gives us a head start on who we want to be."

Charissma stood by admiring Shaunice's enthusiasm for science while talking to the two students. As Shaunice made her way back to the science booth, Charissma uttered, "Sometimes I wish I was as smart as you. Maybe then I'd actually be happy to do this extra-curricular stuff."

"Rizzy, now you stop that!" Shaunice snapped. Charissma knew that Shaunice only called her Rizzy when they were at home. It was a nickname that only her family used and usually meant something important was about to follow.

Before Shaunice could continue, Charissma took out her notebook to prove to her friend that she had a reason for saying that she wasn't smart. She had not passed her Chemistry exam.

"Look at my test results. I got a 55! Do you think I'm smart enough to stay in the STEAM program with grades like this? If I get kicked out of this program, I'll probably never make it to medical school." Charissma let out a huge sigh.

"One bad test grade doesn't make you dumb, Rizzy. Why don't you come over to my house later so we can start studying together? Don't worry best friend, I've got ya!"

Chapter 2

The Kitchen Chemist

Shaunice and Charissma rode the bus together to Shaunice's house, after school. Normally, Charissma always rushed home to babysit her younger sisters, but today her mother was home early from work so Charissma was free to spend the afternoon with Shaunice.

"So after we're done with high school, you were thinking about medical school?" Shaunice asked Charissma. Even though Charissma wasn't too confident about being in the honors program, Shaunice knew that all she needed was a little push to keep her spirits up. Shaunice was also happy that her friend was in the same program as she was.

"Well, my mother expects me to get a job as soon as I graduate but I've been thinking about going to college. I've always dreamed of being a doctor so I know I have to keep my grades up if I want to get into medical school. I just don't know if—"

"That's a great dream to have!" Shaunice interrupted her before she could finish because she didn't want Charissma to start to doubt herself again. "Well, my family seems to think I'll be taking over the family business, but I like the idea of being my own person and creating my own path." Shaunice's parents owned a small bakery, which has been in the family since her great grandmother Ruby opened it back in the 60's.

"Your family bakery is THEE best! My mom can't go a day without her croissants from Baked by Wallace. Oh, and my sisters and I love those little chocolate cream puffs!" Charissma got hungry just thinking about the Wallaces' bakery. "Can you bake like your parents?"

Shaunice shrugged her shoulders. "I mean, sometimes I look over my mom's shoulder when she bakes at home. It doesn't look that difficult. She basically writes all of her recipes down in a cookbook and follows them whenever she bakes. You know what? It actually reminds me of when we follow the steps in science class like, for our experiments. Wait a minute! Maybe baking a cake is like doing science!" Shaunice threw her hands in the air as if she had just made a new discovery.

"It is?" asked Charissma, rubbing her chin.

"Well think about it. You're mixing a bunch of materials together, wet and dry, a little flavor here and there, heat it all up and BOOM! It's basically chemistry!" Shaunice couldn't believe she never thought to make that comparison before. "So you know what that means right?"

"Um... what?" Charissma asked, a bit confused.

"Well my parents are basically scientists which would explain why I love science so much too!" Shaunice was excited about her little discovery.

"So, since bakers are scientists, you should have no problem taking over the family bakery and being a baker too, right?" Charissma smirked.

"No, no. My plan is to become a professor at a university or a scientist finding important cures. I can't use baking to do that!" They both giggled at the thought of what their lives would look like beyond high school.

****

As the bus came to a stop near Shaunice's house, the girls began making their way down the stairs and noticed a familiar face approaching. It was Danny Robinson, who lived next door to Shaunice, and who was also in the same Honors Graphic Design class as Charissma.

"Does he ever put that camera down?" Charissma whispered to Shaunice.

"Hello ladies! Smile for the picture!" Before the girls could respond, the flash from Danny's camera glared so brightly it nearly blinded them, causing Charissma to miss her last step while getting off the bus. Danny quickly leaped forward to catch her as she stumbled to find her balance.

"I'm so sorry, Charissma," Danny whispered. "Are you OK?" He was completely embarrassed because he thought the girls, Charissma especially, would be impressed with his new camera.

"I'm OK, don't sweat it," Charissma responded.

"Nice camera ya got there, Danny," Shaunice added. "So you're really serious about this photography thing, huh?"

Danny loved playing with all sorts of technological gadgets. He had a garage filled with old computers, video games and cameras and broken devices and was always helping his neighbors and friends repair theirs.

"Well I'm actually putting together a portfolio for my Technology Internship completion that's coming up and I need to include some cool photos to show off my great photography skills. Do you think you ladies can give me a few more poses?"

"Not right now, we're headed to my house because we have a lot of studying to do. Come on Charissma, we're already behind on time!" Shaunice replied, grabbing Charissma's hand.

"Please," he pleaded. "This will only take a minute!"

The girls paused and smiled, "CHEESE!" then hurried along their way. "Thank you," he yelled to them as they walked away. "It's picture perfect!"

Chapter 3

Overcoming My Fears

At Shaunice's house, the girls finished their science study session and were downstairs in the kitchen preparing a snack.

"Well that was a productive afternoon," said Shaunice. "Brad-the-brat kept trying to interrupt us!"

"Hey I heard that!" yelled Shaunice's little brother, Brad, from the living room.

"Aww, Brad's just being a kid," Charissma responded. "He's probably just excited that you're home from school and wants some attention from his big sis."

"I don't know. Maybe." Shaunice stopped what she was doing and stood still. "Did you hear that?" She stared straight ahead in the direction of the opened kitchen window.

"Hear what?" Charissma asked.

"Hmm...never mind. I thought I heard something outside." Shaunice poured two glasses of orange juice so that they could have them with their peanut butter and jelly sandwiches. "So Charissma, how do you feel about your new classes overall? Do you like being in a more advanced class?"

"Well, it's nice to be able to tell people that I'm in an 'honors' program but to be honest, I'm a little worried about the amount of work I'll have to do to keep up. It almost feels like I'll need to be in high school forever and we both know my mom wants me to be done with high school like yesterday." Charissma took a sip of her juice. "Maybe if I go back to my old classes which were easier, I'll feel less pressure and won't have to worry about all of that."

"Uh...if going to medical school is your goal, the STEAM program is definitely going to be better for you. I think you'll be just fine if you stick with it. Remember, being intimidated by something that seems hard isn't a reason to quit. My grandma Ruby always used to say, 'If it was easy, everyone would be doing it!' I can definitely help you study for as long as you need me to and together, we're going to be Science superstars!"

The girls said their goodbyes at the front door and Charissma headed home. Just as Shaunice turned to head back inside, she noticed a glare coming from the shrubs along the side of the house. This time, it wasn't a flash from a camera but what looked like glasses. Before long, she realized there was someone trying to hide behind the shrubs.

"Danny, is that you?" Shaunice asked.

Danny, who lived just next door, had gone to take the trash outside earlier and noticed the girls hanging out in the kitchen. While he rustled through the bushes trying to get a better look at Charissma, he did not realize the girls had made their way to the front door. He quickly stooped down behind a few shrubs hoping they hadn't noticed him as Charissma left.

"Hey Shaunice," Danny stood up slowly, "it's not what you think."

"Were you spying on us?" "No, of course not!"

"Well, explain yourself," Shaunice demanded.

"If I tell you, promise me you won't say anything." "OK, fine. I promise"

"I have a huge crush on Charissma. I never really get a chance to see her outside of school so I wanted to see what she was like. I promise, I'm not a creep."

"Don't worry. I don't think you're being creepy. But how come you never said anything to me about Charissma before? You do know she's my best friend, right?"

"Yes, I'm pretty sure everyone at Huntwood High knows that. I guess I was scared of what you'd say." Danny laughed. "By the way, is everything okay with her? She seemed a little distant in class today," Danny said.

"Well, she has been super stressed out from school and in trying to keep up with her new STEAM honors classes. Also, her birthday is in four weeks and I was hoping that she would bring it up, but she hasn't even mentioned it. I get the feeling that she's not even excited about celebrating it."

"Oh wow, I would have never guessed it. She always looks like she has it all together."

"Yeah well, you can't always judge a book by its cover," Shaunice replied. "What if we did something nice for her? You know, something to make her smile and to feel special."

"That's a cool idea. What did you have in mind?"

"Well," Shaunice said, "she's turning 16 and you know that's a milestone birthday! What if we threw her a surprise birthday party?"

"Count me in! I love birthday parties, especially when I get to be behind the camera!"

Chapter 4

I Just Can't Commit

"Clap, clap, stomp, up, twist...1, 2, 3." Rehearsal instructions were coming from Imani Jophus, captain of Huntwood High's Elite Step team. He was a perfectionist and always made sure his teammates were on beat.

Charissma walked into the gym that afternoon, and noticed that the team had almost finished rehearsals. She had agreed to meet Imani in the gym to work on their project for Honors Music and Art class.

"Charissma, I'm over here!" Imani waved, as he moonwalked towards her, making sure not to crease his brand new sneakers. Imani was one of Huntwood High's most stylist students and took great pride in his sneaker collection. "Are you ready to get to work, partner?"

"Sorry Imani," Charissma said. "I actually came to tell you that we need to reschedule. My Mom needs me to come home straight after school today."

"WHAT? But what about our project?" He cried out. "Come on Charissma, you have to stay. The project is due in like a week!"

Charissma felt like she was letting him down. "I'm...I'm so sorry, Imani. I have to take care of my little sisters today because my mom got called into work on her off day." Charissma stared at the ground because she couldn't look Imani in the eye as she delivered the bad news. "We're still partners though. I promise we'll get it done before the due date!" Charissma had no idea if she could actually keep such a promise, but it seemed like the right thing to say.

"Fine, I understand. Say hi to 'Thing 1' and 'Thing 2' for me," Imani laughed, referring to Charissma's younger sisters.

Just then, someone yelled from across the gym, "Shaunice, I can't believe you're leaving!"

Shaunice and her cheerleading squad had also been using the gym to practice their routines. From the sound of things, it did not sound like practice was going well.

"Let's go see what they're so upset about," Imani insisted, pulling Charissma with him in the direction of the cheerleading squad.

As they got closer, Charissma noticed that Shaunice seemed unwell. This was unusual because Shanice was always the most energetic and cheerful member among the cheerleaders.

"My mother is about to pick me up for a doctor's visit," Shaunice explained to the squad. "Honestly, I'm so drained right now, I don't think I'm going to make it through to the end of practice today. Tanisha, do you think you can take over?"

Charissma immediately recognized Tanisha Parker, who was also in her Honors Math class. She hadn't realized that Tanisha and Shaunice were also teammates.

"Shaunice, everything okay?" Charissma interrupted.

"Hey Charissma. I didn't realize you were in the gym. I don't feel like myself so my mom's coming to pick me up to take me to the doctor." She struggled through a smile. "Do you two know each other? This is Tanisha Parker."

"Yes, you're the new girl in Math class, right?" Tanisha stretched her hand out to shake Charissma's. "It's nice to officially meet you."

"Yeah, I sit behind you in class. You're really good in Math. Like, good-enough-to- be-the-teacher good!"

Imani laughed, "She might as well be the teacher. She's a Math whiz! She tutored me last year and that was the only way I was able to pass!"

"If you ever have any trouble, I'll be glad to help you out, Charissma," Tanisha added.

"Thanks, Tanisha, I might just take you up on that." Charissma turned to hug Shaunice goodbye. "I'm heading to the bus stop now but I want to know you'll be alright. Will you call me later?"

"Sure will. Don't you worry about me! My mom will be here any minute now."

As soon as Charissma was out of the gym, Shaunice turned to the group and whispered, "by the way guys, since you're all here, I wanted to tell you that Danny and I are working on a secret plan to surprise Charissma with a birthday party and we need all of you to help us pull it off!"

Chapter 5

Putting Our Ideas Together

With one week until Charissma's birthday, Shaunice knew she had to get the ball rolling. At her next cheerleading practice, she grabbed Tanisha and pulled Imani away from his step practice across the gym to talk party details. Imani and his friends were usually always in the gym at the same time as the cheerleaders, so this made it easy for Shaunice to get a hold of him.

"So you agree that the party is a good idea, right?" Shaunice asked her friends.

"Of course! I can't think of one person who wouldn't want a surprise party!" exclaimed Tanisha.

"I'm happy to have your help," said Shaunice. "So how should we get started?"

Tanisha answered first. "Last year I helped plan the school's Halloween party and one thing I learned is that with any event, you definitely need money....Money for decorations, money for entertainment, money for food. Don't worry, I'm pretty good with budgets, so I'll make sure we don't get too crazy spending money that we don't have."

"Didn't you also organize a fundraiser last year, Tanisha?" Shaunice asked.

"Yup, I sure did. I like where you're going with this. Consider it done. Oh, do you think you could ask your mom to bake something for us? And what do you think about us having the party right here in the gym?"

Shaunice laughed, "Take a breath, slow down. These are all good ideas but we need to make sure we stay organized if we're going to..."

"FLASH MOB!" Imani interrupted. "I can put together a flash mob. Basically, a bunch of us dancers can get together and jump out in spontaneous dance routines. It'll be a perfect way to surprise her!"

"Oh, I love it!" Shaunice screeched in excitement.

"Charissma and I have been working on our Music and Art project together which has a really cool dance part so I think I could trick her into learning a few extra moves as part of the flash mob grand finale."

"Remember, she can't know about the party! It's a surprise" Shaunice warned.

"Don't worry. I'm a mastermind at keeping secrets. She'll still think we're practicing for our Art project."

A fleet of robots whizzed into the gym catching everyone's attention. It was now time for the engineering students to use the gym to work on their robots. Annie Obolola, the lead student engineer, rode into the gym on her electric scooter. She yelled, "Time's up dancers and dance-ettes. We have the gym now, so please exit stage left."

As the step team packed up to leave, the cheerleaders headed to the school's cafeteria to continue working on their routine. Shaunice, of course, would not be joining them because her mother had come to pick her up early from practice, again. She was so excited about her friends helping with the surprise birthday party that she had almost forgotten that her mother was picking her up early or that she had been feeling sick earlier and needed another doctor's visit. She waved good- bye to her friends and skipped and twirled as she headed towards the gym door.

"Ow, My leg," Shaunice yelled as rotated on her left foot.

Her friends ran to her but by the time they got to her she had already collapsed to the ground, grabbing her leg.

Annie could hear the commotion coming from the hallway just outside the gym and rushed out riding on one of her remote controlled mobile chairs. The friends immediately helped Shaunice off the floor and onto Annie's scooter.

Chapter 6

Will I Ever Walk Again?

The Wallace family stood in the examining room, waiting for the doctor to return with news. Mrs. Wallace approached the doctor when he came in. "We've been here a lot more often lately. Is there a diagnosis this time?"

"Shaunice has Multiple Sclerosis also known as MS. Her disease affects her brain, spinal cord and her nerves. It's definitely why she has been experiencing so much pain and discomfort over the last few weeks."

"That sounds scary," uttered Shaunice. "How long before it goes away?"

"Currently there is no cure but I know of some treatments and medications that can slow it down and help you deal with the symptoms. I can see you're sad but new discoveries are being made all the time. It's important to stay positive." Dr. Jones was one of the best doctors in the field and the Wallace family knew they were in good hands.

After their visit to the doctor's office, the Wallace family arrived home to find Charissma waiting at their front door.

"Hey Shaunice!" Charissma stood up and waved as she say the pulling into the driveway. She waited until Shaunice had gotten out of the car. "I know I asked you to call me later but I couldn't wait and wanted to come by to check on you. Is everything okay?"

"How long have you been waiting out here?" Shaunice asked.

"Why don't you come inside, Charissma," Mrs. Wallace said, knowing that the girls had a lot to discuss.

"You can help me up to my room and I'll fill you in," Shaunice said.

As Shaunice explained her diagnosis to her friend, she hated having to repeat what she'd learned in the doctor's office earlier because it was starting to sadden her. "I won't be able to cheer or move around like I have been if my condition gets worse. Dr. Jones said I need to take it easy while I wait for the treatment to start working."

Charissma did not like to see her friend looking so down. "Well I'm sure it doesn't mean you'll never walk or dance again. I'll make sure we do everything we can to prevent that from happening. Besides, didn't you tell me that I should never let difficult situations intimidate me? You're always helping me whenever I'm having a tough time, so now it's your turn to let me help you."

"I could use the help, especially with carrying my bag and books from time to time."

"I can definitely do that!" Charissma reassured her.

"The doctor said I'll also need some physical therapy and a few extra breaks during the school day. Honestly, it's so much to take in. I don't know if I'm even ready to tell the others about it yet. Can I trust you to keep this a secret?"

"You should already know that all of your secrets are safe with me. That's why we're best friends, remember? No secret nor lie could ever come between us."

As Charissma leaned in to hug her best friend, Shaunice felt a bit more cheerful but also felt a little guilty for not sharing one more secret with Charissma - the birthday party.

****

The next morning, Charissma showed up to the bus stop with lots of papers in her hand.

"Whoa there!" exclaimed Shaunice. "Is that all homework?"

"No. I was actually up pretty early this morning doing some research and I found these articles of athletes and students with MS. I was hoping this would cheer you up. Check it out!"

"Aw, thanks Rizzy. This looks really encouraging." Shaunice leaned in to take a closer look at the articles. "There's a guy here running a marathon even though he has MS."

"Yup, he didn't think he would have been able to but he worked really hard and smashed it! Shaunice, your story could be here too! I'm going to keep doing more research and help you fight this thing once and for all."

Shaunice smiled, "Thanks for the inspiration, bestie. Sounds to me like you have a natural talent for taking care of sick people, Dr. Charissma."

The girls both giggled.

"Speaking of which, Mom and I got into a little argument this morning about that. She thinks medical school would be a waste of time and reminded me that she could not afford it. The only way I would ever get to go is if I got a job to pay for it myself."

"But how can you work and go to school at the same time? Isn't college hard and med school even harder?"

"Exactly. I'll probably have to kiss those big dreams good-bye."

"Well, speaking as your best friend and as your first patient," Shaunice replied, "I recommend you go with your heart. We're definitely going to need lots of good doctors like you!"

Chapter 7

Practice Makes Perfect

Imani's backyard was the perfect place for the group dance rehearsal. Both Imani and his older brother were dancers, so their parents invested in a pretty nice dance floor where they rehearsed often.

Danny and Annie rode their bikes over together. The two usually enjoyed sharing stories about what was new in the technology and engineering worlds since they were so similar. Danny liked putting his gadgets to work and Annie liked building them.

As Imani approached the two, Danny said, "Hey Imani. Do you know Annie? She's in my Honors Graphic Design class. Annie, Charissma and I all take that class together."

Imani greeted Annie. "I remember seeing you with those robots in the school gym the other day. You guys have some really cool stuff!"

"I really do love working with the robots." Annie couldn't help smiling. She couldn't believe that the best dancer at Huntwood High was into her robots. "I'm working on building the most impressive robot the school has ever seen."

"That's cool with me" Imani turned on the music. "But how do you all feel about this robot dance?" Imani started to move and shake while the others laughed and joined in.

When Shaunice and Charissma showed up later, Charissma was carrying Shaunice's backpack and they seemed to be walking very slowly.

Danny went over to help. "What's going on, Shaunice? Are you okay?"

"I just needed a little help getting here today, that's all. What are you guys up to?" "We're working on a..." Imani winked, "school project!"

"According to my calculations," said Annie, "we can build a human pyramid with the guys on the bottom, Shaunice and I balancing on their shoulders and we'll just have to get one more person for the top. Charissma, what do you say? You up for it?"

"Um...sure. Imani, is this part of our Music and Art project?" Charissma looked a bit confused.

"Yes. I convinced a few of our friends to help us out so that we would have the best project in class!" Imani responded. "A human pyramid would definitely get us an A. I would have never thought of including that in the routine, but thanks to our genius engineer, we will have an awesome grand finale."

"For the school project," Shaunice reminded him. "For the school project, of course!"

As the kids snuck Charissma off to dance, Danny took out his camera to record the action. "For my Tech Internship portfolio, I'm going to record the party planning, rehearsals and the big event to display on a big projector in the gym. That way, Charissma will see all of my efforts — I mean, our efforts."

"Oh thank you, Danny. That's a great idea!" Shaunice was glad the plans were coming together so nicely and that everyone was so eager to chip in. She was worried about telling the others that could not be a part of the dance since she knew that Dr. Jones didn't want her doing too much. "Charissma is going to love this surprise!"

****

Shaunice returned for her weekly doctor's check-up at Dr. Jone's office.

"So Shaunice," Dr. Jones said. "I'm happy to see you've been able to get through your daily routines. How are you feeling?"

"Honestly," she replied, "I'm more tired than usual and it's harder to get things done."

"We're going to get you the support you need," he responded. I'm sure your school will make accommodations if you need them. I will have my assistant write a note to your teachers."

"My friends have been helping me a lot too. My friend Annie lets me use an electric scooter that she built herself in engineering class, whenever I'm too tired to walk around school. My best friend, Charissma, even found me some cool articles on treatments for MS. Is there a way I can start my own research for a cure?"

"Why yes, I'm glad you asked. I have some information I can give you to get you started."

They chatted about symptoms and remedies and Shaunice began to feel much more hopeful.

Chapter 8

More Money, More Problems

Tanisha's carwash fundraiser was going well. "Thanks for helping out today, Annie. By the looks of all these cars, I definitely think we washed enough to help cover the cost of decorations for the birthday party." Tanisha smiled as she thumbed through the stack of bills she had collected from their customers throughout the day.

Customers from the nearby neighborhoods began driving away, happy with their squeaky clean cars. Annie, who was helping to keep things organized, handed Tanisha another stack of money. "I haven't had a chance to add it all up yet but I know you're good with numbers and you probably already know exactly how much money our day brought in."

"By my calculations, I'd say two hundred bucks," Tanisha said, rubbing a chin.

"I guess they don't call you the Math whiz for nothing." Annie laughed. "If we start packing things up now, we might just have enough time to make it to the party store and catch this week's sale."

"Ladies, ladies! That's a nice stack of cash you got there!" Danny shouted, as he finished drying off the last car for the day. He walked over to the two girls who had been packing up. "Don't forget to save some of that money for my photography things. I need lighting equipment for my camera, so I hope there's enough money to go around."

"Uh..." Tanisha said, "Is that really a priority right now? Can't you just turn on the gym lights and call it a day?"

"Tanisha, dear friend, I'm afraid photography isn't as simple as you might think. It's a delicate art that combines intelligence, creativity and high quality equipment. So, to answer your question, NO!"

The girls both stopped moving around and gave Danny their full attention. His tone changed completely. Whenever he talked about photography, he became very passionate and sometimes a little too serious. "We need the best photo and video quality for the party and I plan to give this project my very best effort." Danny was also concerned about making a good impression in front of Charissma, whom he very dearly admired.

"Oh Lord no," mumbled Tanisha as she stared down at her phone. She had stopped listening to Danny ramble on about his photography needs and was paying attention to a text message from Shaunice, who was at home working on the birthday cake.

"I might need some money for more ingredients. I've already used up all that I had and it looks like my practice cake was a disaster. It looks like a huge, hard cookie," the text message read. She had no idea that her younger brother Brad had deliberately poured the baking powder down the sink and replaced it with more flour. Brad hid behind the refrigerator giggling to himself as he watched Shaunice struggle to stick a fork into the cake.

Tanisha became flustered.

"T, you okay?" Annie asked.

"We will have to get very creative about this money situation. Everyone's asking for money to get things done for the party. Danny needs more lighting, Shaunice needs ingredients for the cake." Shaunice took a deep breath, "It'll be fine. I'm sure we will figure it all out somehow."

"Absolutely, we've got this!" resolved Annie. "Nothing a little creativity can't solve. Don't forget that you're working with the best of the best on this. If we can get through these crazy STEAM classes, we can definitely figure out a way around this challenge."

Just then, Imani ran into the yard, excited and out of breath, dressed in his matching sneakers, hat and basketball jersey. "Outfits! We all need matching outfits for the dance! I should have thought of this sooner!"

Danny and Tanisha both looked at Annie and they all laughed and said "A little creativity!"

Chapter 9

Don't Ruin The Surprise

The students sat at their desks in Science class working on a chemistry problem as Mr. Joseph walked around the classroom checking their answers.

"Mr. Joseph," Shaunice said, as he approached her desk. "I've been giving it a lot of thought and I think I've decided what my research topic will be for our end-of- year report," said Shaunice.

"Great. What topic did you pick?"

"I'm going to work on neurochemicals in the brain and how they control the body."

"Excellent, Shaunice! I'm sure we can all learn a lot from that topic. Now, who can help with the assignment on the board?" Mr. Joseph returned to the front of the classroom and scanned the room for any raised hands.

Charissma volunteered for the first time ever. "I think I have the answer, Mr. Joseph." As she made her way to the board, she started to remember some of the doubts she used to have about being good at Science. She proceeded anyway and managed to complete the problem, correctly.

****

On the bus home, later that day, Danny tried to encourage Charissma to hang out more outside of school. Charissma and Shaunice, who were both on the bus, were more interested in talking about what happened in Science class earlier that day.

"Good job today, Rizzy," Shaunice patted her on the back gently. "I was so proud of you."

"Well I can't take all the credit," Charissma responded. "After all those hours of us studying together, I finally feel confident in my ability to understand Science. I should be thanking you, actually." The girls smiled and embraced one another with hugs.

"...and scene," Danny interrupted. "I hope you don't mind that I just captured that moment on my camera."

Charissma laughed, "You should have been shooting during my chemistry presentation in class today too! You heard Shaunice, I rocked it!"

"Yes, you did, Rizzy. You sure did!"

"What do you ladies have planned for the rest of the afternoon?" asked Danny.

Whenever Charissma went to Shaunice's house after school, the girls always spent most of their time studying. Tonight was different. "We're taking a break from studying tonight because I miss just being able to hang out with my best friend," Shaunice replied. She also wanted to pick her brain to make sure she had no idea that the birthday party was happening tomorrow. Charissma was just thrilled to have had the evening off from babysitting duties.

"Yeah, we have so much to catch up on. I'm planning on celebrating today's win in class by rewarding myself with a study break!" Charissma said.

"Well, birthday girl," said Danny. "I guess this gives you two reasons to celebrate, huh?"

"Oh, right, my birthday! I guess it does," Charissma replied, covering her face with her hands as if she were embarrassed that she almost forgot her own birthday was tomorrow. "If I wasn't so busy with school, I would have loved a party. Although, I know my mom's way too busy to make that happen and she probably couldn't afford to throw one anyway." Charissma looked a bit bothered.

Shaunice and Danny looked at each other and smirked. Charissma was going to be so pleased with the surprise they had coming tomorrow.

****

Mrs. Wallace was already at home putting the finishing touches on Charissma's surprise birthday cake for tomorrow's big day. After multiple attempts, Shaunice thought it would be best to have her mom make the cake because she knew that Brad wouldn't interfere with her mom baking.

"Ma! We're home!" Shaunice yelled as she swung open the front door. The warm cake smell flooded their noses immediately.

"Hey Charissma, why don't you and Danny head on up to my room? I'll go grab us a few snacks from the kitchen and be right up."

As the two made their way upstairs, Shaunice made a mad dash to the kitchen.

"Ma, she's here!" Shaunice whispered.

"Who's here?"

"Charissma and Danny are both here and I had to rush them up to my room before Charissma could realize that you were in here making her a cake. Quickly, let's put it in the refrigerator so she doesn't see it. I would hate for us to ruin the surprise." Shaunice kept looking over her shoulder just in case Charissma had decided to come back downstairs. She spotted Brad standing in the kitchen doorway, listening to the conversation she was having with her mother.

"What do you want, Brad?" She frowned at him.

"So, you guys are keeping secrets from Charissma, huh?" he made a sneaky face and rubbed his hands together.

"Don't even think about it, dude." Shaunice could barely get her last word out before Brad took off running up the stairs. "BRAD! Come back here!" Shaunice yelled, as she chased him.

Chapter 10

Let's Get This Party Started

It was a beautiful, sunny Friday morning and most of the 11th graders were buzzing about the surprise party taking place later that afternoon.

"Shhh! Hurry, come on," Annie said as her and the rest of the party planners snuck into the gym before the first morning bell sounded.

"So, I already spoke to coach Watson. He said we could get the gym around 3:30 pm today, so we should all meet back here at that time to start setting up," Tanisha said.

"Sounds good! I'll stay with Charissma to make sure she does not get a chance to come over to the gym until you guys are ready," Shaunice added. "Do you guys think you'll have enough time to get it all set up?"

"Yeah, absolutely," Annie said. I'm pretty good at staying organized and according to my calculations, this itinerary I made for the event has every detail down to a science." Annie showed Shaunice the master diagram that she had put together. "See right here," she said pointing to the drawing, "the red dots are people's positions, the arrows show the direction that all the dancers will be moving, and that 'X' is where I need you to stand with Charissma as she takes it all in."

"Where is the world's most awesome photographer standing on this blueprint?" asked Danny, as he wedged himself in between Annie and Shaunice.

"I have a special place for you and all of your equipment. You can set up the video that you made to show Charissma on the projector in this corner, then you can hook up your camera to live stream the entire event on social media in the opposite corner," Annie responded. She spent a lot of time preparing the event diagram and schematics and wanted to make sure that all the details were covered. Structure, order, and logic were exciting to her, and as an engineer, she was in her element.

"I've given all of the dancers their T-shirts already, so we should all be in full costume and ready to perform at go time," Imani added.

"And, since we saved so much money on costumes by going with T-shirts, I used whatever leftover money I had to buy a small gift from all of us to Charissma," said Tanisha, as she opened a small, beautifully decorated box.

The five friends all leaned in and their faces illuminated in awe.

****

The gymnasium was brightly lit up and filled with colorful decorations. The big screen was set and Danny was waiting for the cue from Annie to begin the show.

Shaunice and Charissma were in the locker room talking about Charissma's plans for the weekend. A text message popped up on Shaunice's phone.

"Her sisters and I are here," the message read. It was a message from Charissma's mom. Shaunice had filled her in on the surprise and she was delighted to know that her daughter had such amazing and supportive friends. She wanted to add to the surprise by bringing the girls to the party.

"Wanna grab some ice cream after school?" Charissma asked Shaunice.

"I'd love to, but I'll just need to swing by the gym before we leave to say good bye to the other cheerleaders"

"Of course. Let's do it," Charissma enthusiastically replied.

Just then, Shaunice received a text message from Annie, letting her know they were ready for the big reveal.

Shaunice led the way and the two girls walked down the hallway in the direction of the gym.

****

"SURPRISE!" The gym was filled with cheering, clapping, flashing lights, and laughter as the crowd yelled.

"Wait, what?" Charissma looked around, so confused. "What's going on?" Charissma's jaw dropped and she quickly covered her mouth with both hands. "Mom, what are you doing here?"

Her mother and sisters walked towards her. "Well, your friends have been planning this surprise for you for weeks now and I wouldn't miss it for the world!" Charissma's mom and two sisters hugged her at the same time.

Shaunice made her way up to the stage. "Let's get this party started," she yelled, and on cue, the music started pumping. Groups of students began dancing in place and everywhere Charissma looked, a new students joined the dance routine. It was like a human domino effect. Shaunice made her way down to the dance floor where the others had already begun dancing around Charissma. With two shakes and a twist, she started feeling pain in her leg but before she could grab her leg as she often did, Annie drove up to her in one of her electric scooters.

"The scooter was already part of my blueprint diagram," she laughed. "Get in."

Danny walked over with his camera rolling and captured the moment when the STEAM friends presented Charissma with a beautiful charm bracelet. They each added a charm to remind her of the friendship that they all shared; a stethoscope for Science from Shaunice, a camera for Technology from Danny, a mini robot for Engineering from Annie, a dancing sneaker for the Arts from Imani, and a dollar coin for Math from Tanisha.

Charissma was overcome with emotion. She laughed and cried and finished the night perfectly executing the human pyramid dance routine she had rehearsed with Imani. For the first time in a long time, she felt like her future looked bright.

STEAM Glossary

<u>Arts (the Arts):</u> the study creatively expressing oneself typically through audio, visual, physical or literary work.

<u>Brain:</u> a large organ located in the head which controls the way the body works.

<u>Catalyst:</u> something that is used to speed up a reaction but isn't used up in the reaction.

<u>Chemistry:</u> an area of science involving atoms, elements, compounds and molecules. It usually covers how things react with one another.

<u>Elephant Toothpaste:</u> a giant foaming reaction which typically breaks down hydrogen peroxide (H_2O_2) and a catalyst (yeast) into water (H_2O) and oxygen (O_2). It is so big that it that may look like toothpaste for elephants.

<u>Engineering:</u> the use of designs, structures and patterns to organize and build.

<u>Exothermic:</u> to give off heat (the opposite of endothermic reaction, which means to absorb heat).

<u>Experiment:</u> to conduct a scientific procedure which will help to answer a question.

<u>Mathematics (Math):</u> the science of numbers, patterns and shapes.

<u>Multiple Sclerosis (MS):</u> a disease of the central nervous system (brain and spinal cord), where the immune system slows down communication between the brain and the rest of the body.

<u>Neurochemical:</u> molecules that are responsible for carrying information between the brain and different nerves.

Open House: a place or event which welcomes visitors.

Science: a study of the physical and natural world by hypothesizing, observing, experimenting and drawing conclusions.

Science Fair: an event where science presentations are made.

Spinal Cord: a group of nerve tissue running from the bottom of the skull and down the back.

STEAM: formerly known as "STEM" STEAM stands for Science, Technology, Engineering, the Arts and Math.

Stethoscope: an instrument often used by medical doctors to listen to someone's heart or lungs.

Technology: the branch of science dealing with machinery or other equipment (e.g. computers) used to solve problems.

Research: to look up something or investigate.

Appendix A

The Science of Cake
Baking

Most cakes are made up of a few basic ingredients: flour, water, sugar, butter, eggs and baking powder. These ingredients are mixed together (with a few more flavors added) and placed in an oven to cook.

Cake baking can be compared to doing a science experiment. Just like an experiment, the reactants (ingredients mentioned above) combine to produce a product (the cake).

Below is a short description of how each ingredient used to bake a cake relates to science.

Flour

Flour forms the cake's main structure. It contains glutenin and gliadin which form a protein called gluten. Gluten stretches when it bakes and helps to give the cake its shape.

Water

Water is used to help combine and dissolve all of the ingredients. In science, this is referred to as a solvent.

Sugar

Sugar molecules combine with water molecules, to form strong (hydrogen) bonds which help the cake remain soft and retain moisture.

Butter

Butter (or any other fat source) works by coating the sugar and flour molecules and this forms a smooth creamy batter. When the cake batter is whipped, the cream traps air bubbles, which allow the cake to be fluffy when baked.

Eggs

Eggs are a source of fat but also act like an emulsifier. Think of oil and water. Typically, we do not expect these two things to mix. When the butter and water ingredients in a cake come together, they do not mix unless there is something in the mixture that forces them to stay together. The eggs work as a binding agent and keep the cake's ingredients together.

Baking Powder

This is a rising agent (basic) which is also known as bicarbonate of soda (or baking soda). When it is combined with other (acidic) ingredients in the cake, carbon dioxide gas bubbles are released. These bubbles try to escape the cake and push the cake batter up. This is what we see when the cake rises.

References:
Egby, F. (2019, December 10) The Science of Baking a Cake.
https://medium.com/everyday-science/why-do-cakes-rise-52eeb0337a7c
Hoyt, A. (2017, June 28) How Cakes Work. The Chemistry of Cake Ingredients.
https://recipes.howstuffworks.com/cakes.htm
Sean (2017, March 30) Chemistry is A Piece of Cake — The Science of Baking.
https://theskepticalchemist.com/chemistry-cake-baking-science/
Wade, H. (2018, April 23) The Science of Baking: A Complete Cake Guide.
https://www.clubcrafted.com/science-of-baking-complete-cake-guide/

Appendix B

A Few Jobs In Science

Many scientists are usually believed to wear white lab coats and perform experiments. However, there are many different jobs that do not need white coats. Below is a list of science-related jobs, the places you may find these types of workers and some school subjects that these types of workers may have taken. This list is not exhaustive, but it gives a broad idea of the many kinds of jobs where science is used.

Job Type	Who are they?	School Subjects
Anthropologist	Museum worker, Professor, Zoologist, Lab Scientist, Government worker, Humanitarian	Anthropology, Cultural Studies, Biology, Language, Statistics
Archeologist	Hollywood script writer	Archeology, History, Anthropology, Trigonometry
Astronomy and Astrophysics	Climatologist, Astronomer, Meteorologist, NASA worker, Data Scientist	Physics, Astronomy, Engineering, Earth Science, Calculus
Aviation	Air Traffic Controller, Pilot, Military, Aerospace Engineer, Aircraft Mechanic	Physics, Computer Science
Educator	Teacher, Professor, Librarian, Museum worker	Chemistry, Biology, Physics
Forensics	Crime Scene Investigator, Researcher, Publishing Company, Documentary and Film Series Creator	Chemistry, Biochemistry, Biology, Physics, Literature, Mathematics, Criminal Justics
Law Enforcement/ Law Maker	Safety and Health Officer, Environmental Protection agent, Food & Drug Inspector, Health Scientist, Industrial Hygienist	Chemistry, Biology, Mathematics, Environmental Sciences, Toxicology
Medical Professional	Hospital worker, Nursing home, Physical Therapist, Dental worker, Veterinarian	Anatomy, Physiology, Biology, Chemistry
Pharmacologist	Pharmacist, Medical Drug Developer, Laboratory Technician	Chemistry, Biology, Mathematics
Mental Health	Social Worker, Psychologist, Counselor, Therapist	Psychology, Neuroscience, Sociology, Biology

Job Type	Who are they?	School Subjects
Sports	Physical Therapist	Kinesiology, Anatomy and Physiology, Chemistry, Pathology, Biomechanics
Writer	Science Textbook Writer, Science Journalist	Creative writing, Natural Sciences, Psychology, Sociology

VISIT
WWW.MCBRIDESTORIES.COM
FOR MORE TITLES

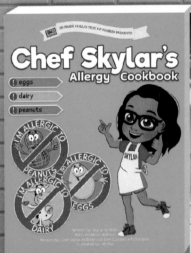

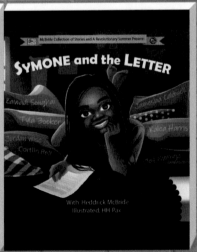

Made in the USA
Middletown, DE
23 November 2020